CONTENTS

DEDICATION

For Matt, Peter, and Devin. Without you, this would have never been writter

———

KIM

September 2004

T he box topples to the floor. Thank God it's the one full of clothes and not the fine china. My cat yowls, skidding into the corner before darting behind the couch. The box must have caught his tail.

'Sorry, Toby.' His amber eyes lock on my feet from his new hiding spot, and I have to sidestep to avoid the wrath of claws.

'It's not my fault the box fell!'

I can't even bother to listen to my tabby's complaints. I'm overwhelmed by a never ending sea of packing tape, suitcases, and boxes.

Kevin adds another and scribbles his name on all four sides with a black marker before adjusting his cricket cap.

'That's the last of mine.'

'Oh, brilliant.' I push hair away from my eyes and look at his clean shaven face. 'Now can you make sure Annie packed?'

My brother scratches the back of his ankle with a trainer. He's older than me by two minutes. We just turned twenty a month ago. Our six year old sister thinks if she doesn't pack, we can't move. I hate to trouble him, but Kevin is her favourite.

'She doesn't understand, Kim.'

'I know.' My face softens. I don't expect her to understand. Since the accident, I've struggled to find the happy medium between big sister and mother figure. How do I go about explaining this? After we lost Mum and Dad, we couldn't afford the house.

Toby creeps from his hideout and moves to the giant windowsill. He's so peaceful in the window watching the sun set. A beautiful contrast of purple, pink, and blue hues contrast the mood inside. I look about the room. Amazing how big a place can become without furnishings. Imprints from the frames, and the nails that once held them, prove we lived here. Tears sting my eyes. No, I can't cry. Kevin can't always be the strong one.

Enjoy it while you can, Toby.

Instead of being broken, I watch the sunset from the back porch a final time.

Poor girl must have worn herself out with all the crying. It's been a long day. When we fetch her, the wee bairn curled on the floor with a pillow and a blanket.

Kevin's shoulders droop before he kneels to pick her up.

'It's better she's asleep for this.

'Are you sure? This'll be the last time she'll see it.'

'It's only two towns over,' he whispers before waking to the car.

'I know, but it's different when the house isn't yours anymore.' I close the door behind me, and slip the key into the letter box. The rational part of me agrees, but the ethical side wants her to wave home goodbye. I look through the window one last time, and will myself to walk away. A lump begins to form in my throat. I go to touch Annie's hair, but my brother stops me. 'No, Kimberly.'

'Kevin, please.'
I swear he can read my mind as the seatbelt clicks.
'She might get upset at first,' he whispers. 'She's been through enough. Don't add this to Annie's list of traumas.'
I turn back round. My hair snags on the headrest, and I close my eyes, and swallow the pain. It can't get any worse. I woke up with a migraine. The kind that starts right at the back of my eyes and spreads to the rest of the head. Not a good way to start the day. Is there a good way to start a day like this? To kiss childhood goodbye and live in the run down, rickety house because it's the cheapest three bed-room for rent in the area? At least none of us will have a last look. Seems fair, eh? Kevin will be busy driving. My eyes are closed, and my baby sister will be in a world of sleep and dreams.
'Let's get this over with,' I mutter.
Kevin's key chain jingles as the engine sputters. Toby's paw hangs out of the crate. I watch our house become smaller, stroking his ginger fur. On any other day, he wouldn't per-mit this, but he's good at reading people. We can't keep our home, but we still have the family cat. He's purring, and that's reserved for Annie.

I hadn't realized we'd been driving until Kevin pulls into the drive. There's no garage, and that makes me uneasy. This town doesn't have a high crime rate, but teens with too much time have the tendency to smash windows. They assume theft and destruction of someone else's personal property is great fun. Why not do it when you know it's dark and the chances of getting caught are slim to none?
Next pay day I'll get one of those signs that read YOU'RE BEING RECORDED and pray the bored little shits don't call my bluff.
Or, we'll get lucky, and the rumours will keep them away.
Kevin smiles and steps out. 'Home sweet home.'
Last time we were here, a few shingles were missing. Some-

one must have done maintenance because it's repaired. I open the door and set the cat carrier down before getting out to stretch my legs.

'Annie will think we live in a castle.' I gaze up at the Victorian home. The roof is triangular. A long porch starts at the steps and extends all the way round to the back.

'Or she'll go hunting for Dracula. Blah blah!' His Yorkshire accent disappears, replaced with faux Transylvanian. 'Blood is the key to everything.'

'Oh, stop. You'll scare her if she hears you talking like that. Your accent is terrible.' We cut our laughter short when Toby meows in the crate. I pick him up and ascend the steps.

'It's safe, Toby.'

Why do I need to reassure him, I don't know. I just need to convince myself that everything will be fine.

The living area has a fireplace. They always looked cosy in the films, but this place makes me uneasy. I'd felt it last time, but I blamed grief. The movers did a decent job with furniture arrangements, but this doesn't feel like home. Or welcoming. We've moved in, but I can't escape the sense we're intruding. Our family pays rent, but does that make it ours?

'Kim.' Annie tugs the hem of my shirt. 'I want to go home.'

'This is our home, Annie.'

At least until Kevin and I become more financially stable.

She gazes at me in stunned silence. Poor Little Dove has been doing that a lot. According to the therapist, it's just shock and will fade with time. Her tiny head touches my hip as she shakes.

'Oh sweetheart.' I run my fingers through her long, brown hair. Just like Mum used to when we cried. 'It's okay to cry.'

She's too young to be without Mum and Dad. I'll never be able to comfort her like our mother did, but I'll be damned if I don't try.

'You don't have to hide it.' My voice cracks, and tears come. This time, I don't stop. I hear Kevin set a box on the kitchen table. He puts his arms around us. For the first time since the funeral, we cry together.

◆ ◆ ◆

The next day goes by uneventful. All unpacking and debates on who gets to stay where. I'm in the room by the staircase.

My bedroom is an icebox. The landlord warned us the house was drafty, but this is absurd. I place the box near the bed and check the window.

No cracks, no draft.

Odd.

The heat needs to kick on. It can't be cold all the time.

"Kim?' a voice calls, as I unpack my figurines.

'In here, Kev! Careful! The last step is a wee bit loose!'

'What?'

Kevin stops and pokes his head through the doorframe. I could've sworn he was downstairs.

I tilt my head. 'Where have you been?'

'The attic. I wanted to check no little creatures were running about. Found some droppings near the entrance. Didn't find any mice though.'

'Did you call me?'

'No, but Annie's in the kitchen.'

'Oh. It must have been kiddo, then.'

'Little Dove's hungry, and I'm starving. What do you say we take a break and get on with dinner? Get our energy up and all that?'

'Sounds good.'

Kevin hooks his arm in mine and leads me to the staircase. I glance over towards the attic door. Something about it isn't right. It's like I'm under surveillance.

'Do you believe the rumours? About the woman and the baby?'

He shakes his head, walking down the steps.

'Since when do you believe in ghosts, Kim?' He snaps, and that takes me aback. Kevin's not one to just lose his temper. Even under the most stressful situations. 'It's a new place. It'll be weird. Enough! At least for now. The last thing we need is Annie getting nightmares. It's an old house. People talk. That's all.'

Something smacks against the window so loud we jump and rush to investigate.

'What the hell?' Kevin, being an athlete, arrives first.

'Did someone throw something?' I join him and peer out the curtains. There's a bird laying in the grass.

'Poor bloke. Must have broken its neck.'

'yeah...'

'Death follows us wherever we go.'

'Can't escape it.' Kevin shrugs. 'We all go someday.'--Sorry.' He runs a hand over his face. 'Guess I'm tireder than I realised.'

'It's okay.'

He's right. I'm being paranoid.

Something breaks in the kitchen.We both jolt and see Toby running off. One of the ceramic decorations that came with the house is splintered into a thousand pieces.

'I'll get a tea towel. Lord knows where the broom is.' I take the one already draped over the oven and kneel to collect the shards. One gets stuck in my hand. A small droplet of blood rolls down the side of my hand.

'You're bleeding.' Kevin kneels beside me and sweeps up the rest. 'I'll take care of this.'

As the droplets seep into the wood, a faint glow radiates from the floor. When I blink, it's gone. I shake my head

B.L. Koller

and walk to the sink to clean the cut. A trick of sunlight through the window.
Kevin's joke from earlier rings out in my mind. *Blood is the key* sounds ominous when I think about the house's history.

ANNIE

October 2005

The doctor Kim and Kevin try to get me to talk with is nice. In her office, she lets me colour and play with Legos. She even has a dollhouse in the corner. But we haven't played with it. It's okay, I'm not disappointed. I have dolls to play with at our house.

'Still enjoying the mansion, Annie?' Everyone asks that question,but the answer I give is always the same.

'It's okay. It's big. Toby likes it, I think. He has lots of room to run around.'

'But do you like it?' Kim picks off all her nail polish during our visits. Kevin nudges her, but she just keeps going on as if nothing happened.

'I miss our old house, though. But we can go back one day when Kim and Kevin have more money.' Kim bites her lip and Kevin puts a hand on her shoulder. Another Lego gets added to the stack. The four of us are building a castle.

'And how are things at school?'

'I don't like school.'

'Why not?' The doctor scribbles something down on her notepad.

'It's boring.'

Kevin laughs, and Kim nudges her elbow into his ribs. Not

enough to hurt him, but just to scold him. I don't know why she isn't fun anymore.

'Have you made any new friends?' Laura is nice, but asks stupid questions.

'One. He's older. We're only friends cause Lizzy is Branson's nanny.'

'I see.' Dr Laura writes on her notepad.

Lizzy is Kim's girlfriend. She's also sad that Kim is too busy for me. Kim used to play all the time! We went to Kevin's cricket matches, or watched him at the batting nets together. I'd sit on her lap. We'd sit in the middle of the stands because that was the best view. Sometimes we'd even catch a high ball. Now all she does is work. Kevin brings me to his games with him early.

'Kim why don't you come to Kevin's games anymore?' Appointments are the only time we all get to play.

'I...' She avoids giving the answer right away by rummaging through the bin. 'It's not that I don't want to go. I just... I have a lot more responsibilities than I used to, Little Dove. I'll try to come to the next one.'

'Promise?'

'I swear.'

After our visit Kim has to go back to work. Someone named Trevor called out. She said some words I'm not allowed to repeat and broke her promise. I miss her a lot. Kevin and I always go for walks when he's finished with practice. My brother is amazing at cricket! The balls shoot at him like rockets and he hits them almost every time. He also says naughty words Kim says only grown ups can say. It's silly. What makes a word "grown up"?

'Where do you want to go to today, Little Dove?' He picks me up, and carries me on his shoulders.

I tap my chin. 'The old house!'

Kevin's eyebrows crinkle together as he tilts his head.
I take his baseball cap off. I need to keep the sun out of my eyes. His hair sticks out in a bunch of different directions, and he laughs as I try to make it not so messy.
'Aye.'
Kevin says Kim will murder him if I sit in the front seat. So, I say in the back. Leaves have fallen all over the ground. Just a few days ago they were all different colours. Now there everywhere. Some look like they've been there for a million years, all crumpled and gross.

'We can't go inside, but we can reminisce.'
'Huh?' I peek out the window to see our old house.
He raises his eyebrows at me and gives me a sad little smile. 'It's not ours anymore, kiddo. We can think back on the good old days.'
'This is the wrong place. I don't mean our old house. I meant the old, old house!'
'You mean a nursing home?'
'No!' I cross my arms and pout. What is so hard to understand! How can I say it so gets it?
'I don't know what you mean, Annie.' Kevin's shoulders sag. He runs a hand through his hair, and that only makes it even messier and makes the grey stand out.
'It is the house where all the graves are.'
'The house where all the...?' Kevin squints for a moment until his eyebrows raise. 'Oh! You mean that place by the church!'
'Yes!' I clap. Kevin always understands me. Kim used to. Now she only knows how to pretend to be Mummy. She's a better sister than a Mummy. Why can't she be more like Kev and not try to be different? And leave me to go to her rubbish job. Kevin ruffles my hair.
'You sure have some imagination. All right. Let's go see this

house.' He chuckles, and I giggle back at him.

Kevin holds my hand.
'Oi, don't run too fast! This place is old. I dunno how sturdy the floor is. I also don't have the foggiest if this is even legal now that I come to think of it.'
It smells weird in here. The walls are also black in places where it caught fire.
'Hurry, Kevin!' I tug him towards the fireplace. There's a loose brick, but it's hard to pull.
'Annie, what are you doing?' He kneels next to me and takes my hand. It's not harsh like when Kim scolds me. There's laughter in the way he talks.
'There's a secret in there and I need it!'
'A secret?'
Kevin looks from me, to the brick, and then back at me. He smiles and wiggles the brick . It's loose, and just sticks out more than the others. He runs his hands over the others, but they seem to be smooth.
'How do you know about this place? I barely know what you meant.'
'Emma said so!'
'Is that one of your friends?'
I nod.
The wind blows through the cracks. Nobody ever bothered to fix this place when it burned down. But that meant nobody looked for its secrets either.
'If I take out this brick,' Kevin holds out his little finger to me. 'Do you pinky to promise to let us go home and not tell Kim about this little adventure?'
'I promise!' Our pinkies link together and he stands with a grunt. He stretches his arms over his head, and all ten of his fingers make a cracking noise. I hate when he does that.
'What's behind door number one?' He kneels down again

and wiggles the brick out of place.
'I loosened it for you!'
'Aye! You did.' He laughs, and places the brick down.
Before he can do it, I reach in. My fingers touch something. It feels lumpy and worn. I get my hand around it, spin and clutch it to my chest.
'It's just like Emma said! The book is here! The book is here!'
Kevin looks like I've just hit him over the head with the brick he just pulled out of the wall.
'Let me see, Annie.' He holds out his hand, and I stop spinning to hand him my prize.
The cover is brown and held closed by a thick piece of string. Kevin's eyebrows get wrinkly in the space between your eyes and nose. He looks like one of those dogs with the smushed faces.
'I'm not sure we should take this.'
I frown.
'Finders keepers! Losers weepers!'
He pulls at the string and opens up the book.
'It looks like a diary.'
He looks back at the hole where I pulled it from, and flips through a few pages.
"1832! This is ancient."
He stares at me then looks back at the brick before putting it into the proper place.
'Well, whoever owned this won't be coming back for it I reckon. Let's get back to car before I get arrested or something, eh Annie?'
The wind picks up again, and my whole body shivers.
'Yes The car is warm. And we have the book! Just like Emma said.'
Kevin still has that look on his face like he's trying to understand. When we're back in the car, Kevin flips through the journal. The handwriting is old, and the pages smell like dust and smoke, but the ink is still easy to read.

15

'The bricks protected it from damage.' He mutters as he runs his hand over one page.

'What does it say Kevin? Can you read the loopy letters?'

'Today I discovered I am with child. I'd say that this comes as a complete surprise, but I am not so prudish as to believe that it is unexpected.' Kevin's face turns red, and he shuts the book.

'What is Prudish?'

'It's a fancy word for proper.'

His face is still red.

'Kevin, are you sick? Is that why your face is all red.'

'Aye!' He blurts. 'Allergic to the dust.'

Something in how he says this tells me that my brother is lying.

KIM

November 2005

I 'm running late. The coffee is bitter, and it burns. We needed to be out the door two minutes ago.

'Annie,' I call upstairs, tapping my foot. 'I hope you're ready. You'll miss the bus if you're not here soon!'

I only get a high pitched whine, but at least she is awake enough to let me know she didn't just crawl back into bed after breakfast.

'No winging! Don't make me call you again.'

Something feels like it's missing, and I take a second to realise I've left the cheese toastie in the kitchen.

'Oh, bugger!' I hurry over, grab the brown paper bag on the table, and double check that Annie's name is on it. She'd never eat Kevin's tuna melt. Then there're feet running across the hardwood floor. Annie comes into view and somehow takes two steps at a time before jumping the last three. The new found parental part of me wants to scold her, but the sister half can't help but look impressed. She steps into her shoes while I slide the oversized coat over her shoulders.

Kev and I used to do that all the time when we were Annies age. Now it seems we've passed the traditions onto her.

'Have a good day at school!' She shoots me a look and I can't help but laugh as I kiss her cheek.

'Kevin will be home to fetch you off the bus. I should be home around seven to make dinner. I love you.'

'Love you too.' She wraps her arms around my leg then scurries out the door just in time.

'In a bit Kim.' Kev checks his keys are in his pocket, and grabs lunch off the counter. He is in his work uniform and it's so weird to see him without that cap, and cricket jersey. It's one of the few jobs he can get that'll work with the hours he needs to be home by. He kisses my cheek, and a minute later the roar of his motorbike tells me he's off. I can't stand that thing, but it solved the car problem.

With everyone else taken care of, I hurry on and get ready for job number one. House cleaning. we take what we can get.

It's been a long day. My shoulders ache, and I'm sure I have bruises from when all those soup cans fell on me while restocking the shelves at the mart.

I must overwork myself. Or maybe I'm already asleep and this is some dream my brain has come up with. I'm staring up at the ceiling and I watch what appear to be shadows move across the room. But they don't move organically. They swirl, no, they glide. That would be the more appropriate adjective. Whatever they are, I don't like them. There's something sick in how they move.

'I told Kevin to take the rubbish out,' I mutter to myself as I cover my nose. I'm still in my pullover. It doesn't matter how high I crank the heat. This room is cold. It's tempting to just curl up on the sofa. Stay by the warmth of the fire. My bedroom door squeaks open and I pray to the god I don't believe in that the noise doesn't wake Kevin. Though, he'd deserve it for not taking out the rubbish. It stinks to high Heaven. How the stench has found its way into my room, I don't know. Maybe the rubbish bin is close to a vent or something.

'Kim?' It's high pitched. Too high to be Kevin's.

'Annie, what are you doing up? Bad dreams?'

When I turn nobody is there. I flick on the light just to make sure. Then Conclude my sleep deprived, stressed out, brain must be overloaded. I'll get myself upstairs as soon as I rid this house of that horrid stench. I dunno what my brother has slipped into the bin. Whatever it is, it's rancid. The lid opens when I step on its lip, only to find I owe Kev an apology.

'it's empty.' So what is making that terrible stench? Whatever the cause, it seems to have faded. Or my nose has just adapted to the smell. I trot up the stairs with surprising speed.

Just get back to the bedroom. My slippered feet are thudding against the floor. Like a child, I reach for the door and keep it open a crack so the light from the hall seeps through.

We've been here for more than a year. These feelings should have faded by now. Then the smell hits my nose, causing me to dry heave into the palm of my hand.

I snatch up a scarf from the coat rack and tie it around my mouth and nose. That at least makes it somewhat bearable. Or at the least livable for a night until I can figure out what the hell that is.. Something compels me to bend down and look under the bed.

'Oh that is disgusting!'

There's a family of dead mice slumped together under my bed. I've nothing to put them in. But they can't stay. Goose flesh prickles my arms and the hair on the back of my neck stands on end. It's so bloody cold and I don't understand why.

I need a broom or something to sweep up under my bed. Which means I must trek all the way back down to the kitchen.

B.L. Koller

The thought terrifies me, but the longer I stay here the smell gets worse. Not even the scarf can block it out now.

I hurry to my feet and grab the rubbish bin from my desk and rip the scarf from my mouth just in time for sick to get caught up in it. Dammit, Kim get hold of yourself! It's just a few dead mice. No need for dramatics. But even after I've emptied my stomach the feeling doesn't go away.

And is it my imagination, or can I see my breath? I put the bin down and snatch the plastic bag inside. Now I will have to go back and march back to the kitchen. The door creaks more, and Toby's shadow cuts across the room. I can see his tail straight up in the air.But when I turn to face the door, it's not Toby standing there making the shadows.

A woman stands in the doorway. Feet not touching the ground. Her hair has fallen all round her face. But I can still see those black, lifeless eyes.

'Kimberly,' it whispers as the sick bag hits the floor. She has a smile on her face but everything about this woman looks off. Her hair hovers out as if she is floating in water. It stretches her mouth in an eerie, inhuman smile. It's too long. The skin shouldn't be able to stretch like that. But it's her laugh that does me in.

Laugh is a generous term. It's more like a cackle. And now that I can see her teeth, their rotted and swollen. They appear to be much too large for her mouth. And it's so high pitched I have to cover my ears. I drop to my knees, and scream.

'Kim?' Kevin rushes in. He runs straight through the woman. When I blink, it's as if she never there. Kevin's arms wrap around me and I bury my face into his chest.

'You ran right through her, Kev!'

'Ran through who?' He looks over his shoulder to find just an empty hallway.

'The woman! How could you not see her?'

He shakes his head and covers his mouth with his arm.

'Oh that smell is awful, Kim!' His eyes fall to the sick bag, and he looks at me with concern. A hand goes to my forehead.

'I could have sworn...' I look into the hall. Kevin stands and picks up the soiled bag.

'That smell can't just be from the gip.'

'I found a family of mice under my bed. Their dead. How could we have not bothered to look? We knew this place had a pest problem.'

'You go brush your teeth and freshen up a bit. I'll take care of the mice.'

'I don't want to go it all alone Kev. Please come with me. Please. This house is creepy and everything has gone to shit! All I wanted to do was get some bloody sleep, and this is what I have to deal with on top of everything else!'

'It's okay, Kim. I promise. Okay, I'll come with you to get yourself clean. You work yourself too thin.'

It was just my mind trying to work out sleep deprivation and the smell of decay. It must be.

I thought Annie could use a playmate, and when Mrs Rodgers gave Lizzy the green light to bring him over, I figured out why not kill two birds with one stone? Someone at least a wee bit familiar. It broke my heart to see her just play tea party by herself. I don't get to see my girlfriend often. We're both busy.

'Afternoon love.' She pecks my cheek and lets go of her cousin's hand. She looks after him on weekends while his parents sell at the local farmers market.

'I brought doughnuts!' Lizzy opens the lid of the take away container, holding it towards me.

'You live in the spooky house?' The boy is seven, but is tall for his age.

'It's not that spooky,' Annie pushes me aside to hug them.

'Branson,' Lizzy scolds as he reaches for the box. 'I told you!

No more doughnuts. Three is more than enough.'
'No,' he beams. 'The box is still full up, Lizzy.'
'And they aren't all for you, little man.' She ruffles the mass of sandy blonde curls and laughs.
'Off to the kitchen, you lot.' I say, taking the box from her.
'The kettles on.'
It's a mystery how the kid stays thin. He never stops eating. Toby meows from his bed in the corner, and runs over to the both of them, watching something out of the corner of his eye. Annie scoops him up, and smiles at Kev when he walks through the door.
'Ey up! Look who's here!' Kevin grabs a doughnut, before putting it in the cabinet.
"I just got the game system set up. Why don't the three of us go play, eh kids?"
'Is it the racing game?' Annie's eyes light up.
'It sure is! C'mon, let's go play!'
I smile at him as the kids giggle. Lizzy chuckles and takes my hand before walking towards the staircase. I freeze.
'Kim?'
'I… we… We can't.'
'I just thought we could go talk? That's all.' She tilts her head and glances up the stairs.
'It's…' I glance over my shoulder, and the noise from the game in the living room fills my ears. I know she's supposed to be watching the kid, but I want to go for a walk. Just like old times.
But old times fade.
'I'm just being foolish.' I smile and nod towards the steps. If Lizzy comes with me, maybe she'll just stay away. I caught her watching from Kevin's window as I left for work the other day. It sent a chill down my spine.
'You're tired,' Lizzy remarks as we walk up the steps.
'I can't sleep.'
My heart pounds as we approach my bedroom. I can still see her floating. How nothing looked right.

My fingers hover over the doorknob a few seconds before she clears her throat and I find the courage to turn it. The door squeaks. I recoil.

'You really are sleep deprived. Don't tell me you've started to believe the rumours! Is that what has you so on edge?'

'No,'I collapse onto the bed, trying to sound nonchalant.'Just got a lot on my mind. That's all. I don't know how I will pay for those bloody dance lessons but I don't have the heart to tell Annie she can't go anymore... And then there are the other bills.' I put my arm over my eyes so I don't have to stare up at the ceiling. That's another thing I see all the time now, sailing shadows. Things that don't belong here.

The mattress sinks, and Lizzy wraps her arms around me.

'We'll figure it out. And I can help pay for her lessons.'

'That's your money, Liz. I can't take it.'

Lizzy tucks a strand of hair behind my ear and kisses my nose.

'Go to sleep, then we can talk about whatever is bothering you.'

It's not an order, but I listen anyway. It's the first time I've ever felt at peace in this stupid room, and I will not waste it.

I tell her what I saw the other night. It's met with skepticism.

'I've never been one to believe in this stuff. You know that. But I know what I saw. '

Lizzy holds up a hand and pats down my hair.

'You've been through a lot. It makes sense that you'd want to believe in ghosts. I think you should talk to someone, Kim. I'm worried. Therapists aren't just for children who lost their parents. They work fine for twenty one year olds too.'

This whole situation is frustrating. I know I'm not going mad. Not even Kevin believes me. Is here anyone I know of that believes?

A thought hits me.

Trever believes in the paranormal. He does those Tarot readings and shit! I'll chat with him about all this.

When I break for lunch, I find him in the breakroom. Trevor's hair is now a rich raven black. The wig looks hideous, but it'll allow him to keep his job. He'd come in yesterday with a neon green hair, and the boss demanded that he make it a "natural" colour. I take a seat beside him.

'Hey Trevor, I need a favour. You believe in ghosts, yeah?'

He takes a sip from his travel mug and raises a brow. 'I do.'

'I think I'm starting to. But everyone I've spoken with has written me off. Lend me an ear?'

'Aye! I'm always happy to hear about an haunting.'

' You can help me draw her out, then. As far as I know, she only comes out of the room to see me. My girlfriend and brother don't listen, and if I ask my little sister, it might just frighten her.'

'Ah.' He smiles and offers me a cigarette. I shake my head.

'Then a ghost hunting we shall go! But first, Let me give you a tarot reading. If you'll have me, I'm free this Saturday?'

Saturday works best for me.'

He nods and leaves with his travel mug and a cigarette between his lips.

KEVIN

October 2005

I run my fingers over the Journal. The front page has a name, or at least it did at one time, but even though the book is well preserved, it's still old and faded, making it impossible to read certain parts. A lot of the pages towards the front have been either torn out, or came loose and are still hidden away in that wall. Otherwise, it's pretty well preserved. Some pages are water stained, but not illegible. I've been trying to piece things together as to how or why Annie would want something like this. Nothing unusual inside. Just a woman's day to day life. Shame she never makes mention of her name. I could see if her name is on any of the tombstones. Maybe leave the diary with her. I hoped to find some sort of answer to why it was hidden away. What made this worth hiding in the bricks?

'Kevin?'

'With you in a moment!' I toss the journal in a drawer before walking to the door. If Kim is calling, I'm not keen on explaining why I have an old leather-bound journal. Or that I took Annie to that old house this afternoon. Kim is on the bed attempting to knit. Dunno much about needle arts, but it looks a little lumpy. Her cheeks are puffed, and her eyes narrow. I reckon it isn't going the way she planned.

'Bit paggered, eh Kim?'
Her head snaps up and she tosses the needles to the edge of
the bed and flops down.
'The tutorials make it look so simple!'
I chuckle and lean on the doorframe. 'What'd you need?'
'I heard some noises in the attic. Somethings up there, and I
don't want more dead things under my bed. Can you go and
have a look? Still don't like going in there.'
'Aye, I'll do it now. Thought I heard something too, this
morning. Can't hurt to have a look.'
'Thank you, Kev. I owe you.' She flashes me a smile. I turn to
go and hear her sigh. I may not be able to see her with my
back turned, but I can tell her smiles dropped.
'Don't be so hard on yourself, Sis.' I call before opening
the attic door. The knob is cold to the touch, and the door
creaks on the hinges when pushed. The wallpaper is faded.
It could do with an update. A word with the landlord is
in order. A fresh coat of paint here might make Kim less
weary. There's a cobweb in the corner, but it's out of my
reach. Too deep in the rafters, even with a broom. In the
corner, there's a rickety rocking chair, but I doubt that
will support my weight. And those things aren't the most
sturdy. My eyes fall on the dusty old leather chest that
came with the house. Always wanted to have a look inside,
but the landlord doesn't have the key.
'That'll do.' It's lighter than expected, but whatever is in
there shifts when I pull it. I grab the broom, step up, and
mop up the cob web. When I step down, and turn back to
the rocking chair, a crow is perched on it, tilting its head at
me.
'Ey up. How did you get in?' The bird just blinks at me, and
caws before flying up to the wood where the web had been.
'Guess this explains the noise. You got a nest up here?'
What am I doing? Having a nice right chat with a crow. As if
it can offer me an answer.
' Key!' It says, peering down at me with black eyes.

I jump back and stick a finger in my ear.

'Come again, Mate?'

It caws again, and disappears deeper into the roof. I squint, trying to find the hole our uninvited flatmate has run off into. Farther back in the attic, something clinks against the floorboards. Curious, I walk towards the sound. Much to my surprise, there's an old metal key on the floor. The dark colour matches the chest.

'Key?' The crow croaks again before flying out the open window.

'This is madness.' I run a hand over my face before bending down to pick up the key. This day continues to get all the more strange. I toss the key in the air a couple times, debating if I should let curiosity get the better of me. Still undecided, I close the window, and hope that for now, that'll be good enough to keep the crow out. I stare at the trunk, and drum my fingers on the sill.

'Ah, what the hell? Could be just old clothes for all I know.' The key fits perfectly, and makes an audible click when I turn it in the lock. Just like the door, it creaks open. At first, there's little that would be of interest. An old knife, rusted with age. Some torn up white fabric, and a yellowed, lightweight dress.It smells like mothballs. When I pick up the fabric, a book that must have been tucked inside falls. At first I assume it's a bible, but instead of a cross, there's a star carved into a circle. When I open it, there's an inscription in the front in red ink.

S. Elisabeth Stewart.

Just like the journal, it's a little faded, but all things considered well preserved. I turn it over, only to find the back is blank.

This house dates back to the late 1890's. I wonder if this is one of the things that got left behind. There's still a bookmark sticking out. With a shrug, I open to the marked page.

'summon death. What a load of rubbish!' Tucking the book

under my arm, I nudge the lid closed with a foot before locking the crate.

'Don't' There's a whisper in my ear, and I'm greeted by an overwhelming chill. I shake my head. The wind pushed open the window again. I close it again, this time making sure the latch works before returning to my bedroom to take another look at that journal. When I catch a glance of myself in the mirror, I notice there's four red lines on my arm. Must have happened during practice.

SARAH

December 1893

I've been talking out loud to myself quite often. Thunder rolls in the distance as I add another log to the fire. I wrap my shawl tighter. Even though the cabin is made of stone, it doesn't hold heat very well. A muff warms my hands.

'It must be done tonight.' I stare at my reflection. My hair is a knotted mess. How am I supposed to tuck it up in this state? and it doesn't matter how much rouge I apply. My face is still too pale. Tonight? It seems early. But they'll be looking for me. I can't go home to Edward. He'll deem me a sinner and turn me away. My boots echo off the walls as I turn away from the mirror. I resemble her well enough to pull this off. But Emma would never consider this. I look down to see my hands trembling. After I lost the baby, I didn't have the heart to tell my poor husband. My sister, Emma also happens to be with child. The both of us hadn't planned on being pregnant at the same time, but this is God's will. I'd considered other options, like an orphanage. But they would also know my face. Would they bring me back to that awful place?

'For the hundredth time, how would that look? And even if that plan could work, there would be a paper trail! They keep *records*, Sarah.' Still, this isn't right. Has desperation driven me so far? No, if such matters were frowned upon, they wouldn't exist. Magic has been practiced for centuries! It's only recently that it has been deemed unholy. The ones who forbid it are the real sinners. Yes. Hypocrites the lot of them. Partaking in sences and contacting the dead. How is that any different?

Who else could I speak with other than myself? Nobody could possibly understand. And I need to stay hidden. I can't get locked away in that place again. Even the Coven has turned on me. But I've come this far. I might as well get on with it. If I'd been honest with Edward, none of this would have to happen. It's my own cowardice that has led me down this path. And I've gone too far to end it now. Emma will be coming tonight. I need her to.

'My sister is not my friend.' It sounds so cold, but sometimes the truth has ice to it. I turn back to the mirror, and take a deep breath. She's the only person I trust. I glance over in the corner. An old chemise sits in pieces. I've torn the cheap muslin fabric apart and stuffed it with bits of leftover fabrics. Appearances are everything. I light a candle, and read over my book a final time. When I look out the window the clouds have darkened, as the winds pick up, I wonder if it will be cold enough to snow?

KIM

December 2005

'**I**'m home,' I call to nobody in particular as I walk towards the kitchen. Annie is at the table eating a bowl of Frosted Flakes and listening to something. From the sounds of it, it sounds like an audiobook. Mum and Dad read to her all the time. She loved it. It's a shame we don't have more time to read to her, but she never complains. Maybe she liked the narrators more than us. Whatever the reason, I'm relieved she's content with them.

'Cereal isn't dinner, Annie.'

Annie shrugs and plops another spoonful into her mouth. I walk over to her and give her a hug before crossing to the fridge and grabbing a jar of tomato sauce.

'Let's make spaghetti. I know it's your favourite!'

I glance over my shoulder to see her nodding in agreement. Not as enthusiastic as I'd hoped, but some response is better than none.

The audiobook stops as I grab the box of pasta from the cabinet.

'Kim?' Annie's bare feet make a noise as she slides them across the floor.

'Hm?'

'Can we go shopping?'

I rummage through where we keep the pots and pans and plop one that seems to be an appropriate size for three servings of pasta on the stove.

'What kind of shopping?' Maybe she misses the snacks. I really should get in the habit of using coupons.

'Dress shopping.'

My heart sinks. maybe I can take her to the second hand shop. Do six-year-olds know the difference?

'One day, of course. But at the moment, we're a little short on money, little dove. But as soon as we can promise, we can go out dress shopping!' I say with as much enthusiasm I can muster. I've never been a fan of dresses myself. Come to think of it, neither has Annie... An odd request.

'What brought this on? I didn't think you fancied dresses.'

'Yes but I saw Emma wearing one, and it was so pretty...'

Her imaginary friend again? I was hoping she'd outgrown those. The way her shoulders slump makes my heart shatter even further. With all the dance wear she's seen I can hardly blame her. Everyone looks so elegant in the classes before hers. And she's so young. They must look like princesses and queens to her. A lightbulb goes off in my head.

'Lizzy can teach you to sew. You can make your own dress I'm sure.' I wouldn't tell her that the fabric she can use is one of the old bedsheets, but I want to see her excited about things again, and if I continue to deny her too often, she'll start to resent me. I can't allow that to happen.

Her eyes light up and her arms are around my leg in an instant.

'Really?'

'Yes.' I laugh and ruffle her hair. 'But you have to promise to pay attention and listen to Lizzy *very* carefully. Needles are sharp.'

'I promise!'

'I'll talk about it with her tonight, then.'

'Thank you, Kim! I love you!'

'I love you too, Little Dove.'

Lizzy came over with heaps of hand needles. There's a sewing machine in the attic, but I can't go up there. The energy in my room is the worst at night, but every time I pass that bloody staircase, I get the sense that the attic is *hers*. It is not a place for me to go. And the last thing I want to do is piss her off. For the most part, she's been civil. I don't think she's slipped into my head. Maybe I'm just being silly. Perhaps there is a way that the two of us can live harmoniously. And maybe all she wants is company. I can imagine it probably get lonely here. I didn't even believe in any of this stuff before I moved it. It sounds a bit cliche, but maybe that's just because it's true. That whole seeing is believing thing.

I tap away at my keyboard from the living room. Trever should be coming over as well. He says he wants to do a test reading. See if he can sense something. The doorbell rings,

B.L. Koller

and it echoes through the entire house, it nearly makes me jump out of my skin.

'Just a moment, please!' I call from the room, hoping that I'm loud enough to hear. I stand, and look at the clock. I thought I heard it chime, but as I walk past the staircase, it seems more like a crying of sorts. Kevin is out, so that leaves him out of the equation. Liz and Annie are in the kitchen and giggling. So, does that mean *she* is the one crying? If so, Trevor has impeccable timing.

I stand on my tiptoes and peer out through the peephole in the door. Sure enough, in all his neon haired glory stands Trevor. It seems he's brought the first flurries of snow with him as well.

'Hey, C'mon in!'

Trevor smiles and steps inside before hanging up his coat and scarf up on the nearby coat rack. He pauses and turns towards the staircase. So, I'm not the only one that's noticed it, then? Or maybe the two of us are both just completely mental. Though, somebody else taking note of the weeping noises from the attic helps to put my mind at ease.

Toby comes running, and drops a mouse at my foot, and meows victoriously. Could I have mistaken the squeak of a mouse for a weeping noise? It seems possible.

'Well, that's lovely.' I sigh and cast Trevor an apologetic look. My cat dropping a dead mouse at my feet would have not been on my list of great moments.

'Oh, it's fine. I had a cat that did the same thing with chipmunks.' He kneels down and holds out a hand. My eyebrows raise as Toby gives him a whiff, and his little pink

34

tongue rakes across Trevor's thumb.

'Impressive.' I say over my shoulder as I cross to go get a broom. It's better to rid the house of evidence before Annie can see it. 'He's not usually the type to cosy up to strangers.'

'Cat's tend to like me.' Don't have the foggiest idea why. I'm just an average Lad. For creatures with unusually high standards, they certainly lower them for me.'

I don't know him well enough to confirm or deny that fact, so I simply don't acknowledge it. I reemerge with a broom, and sweep the mouse towards where the rubbish bin. I pick up the poor thing with a paper towel by the tail and toss it in the bin. Not much else I can do with it. It's too late now. And maybe this is my punishment for renting a house where they were upfront and honest about the rodent problem. If only they'd been more upfront about the lady who lurks in my room, and the attic. I return and offer Trev something to drink. He denies it, and we venture out into the living room. It's chilly, but that's nothing new.

'Make yourself at home.' I begin to toss logs into the fireplace.

'Uh, thank you.'

There are newspapers that we piled up in a neat stack. Either Toby, or my phantastic flatmate are to blame. With a sigh, I pick them up, and stack them again before pulling a few pieces from the paper, crumpling them into balls, and tossing them in with the wood. I strike a match, ad drop it near one of the crumpled bits of paper. In a satisfying sort of way, it catches, and the wood makes this sort of popping noise before that too catches, and within a few seconds, the fire is ablaze, and the room at the very least is heating up. At this point, I'll take any bit of improvement I can get at this point. Satisfied with the fire i've started, I stride over towards the couch and plop down next to him. s

'So,' I rub my hands together. Damn the poor circulation in my hands. Consistently cold no matter what I do. 'How do we go about this?'

Trevor smiles and pulls out that same velvet bag. 'I think the easiest thing to do would be to figure out what your specific card is. Every person has a card that calls to them. Or so that's how the Tarot traditions go.'

He pulls the cards from the bag, and knocks on the top of the cards. I must look pretty curious, because he's quick to offer some sort of explanation.

'That's called knocking on the deck. It Sorta...' He swirls his hand in the air as he searches for the right words in his head. 'I guess you could say that it kind of awakens the deck. That's the easiest way I can think of to explain it.'

Trever passes the deck to me and I raise an eyebrow at him.

'I haven't any idea how to use this.'

'I'll guide you through it. But all I need you to do for the moment is shuffle the deck.'

It feels strange in my hands. They are a bit bigger than the standard deck of playing cards. Just the cards face down are beautiful. A black background decorated with yellow twinkling stars. Very reminiscent of the nights sky. I shuffle the deck and await further instruction. He takes the deck from my hands, and fans them out.

'Choose which one calls to you the most.'

I blink. 'How will I know which one calls to me?'

'It's different for everyone. Hold out your left hand and just wave it over the cards. Some people feel like their cards are warm. Others report a tingling sensation. Either way, I'm confident you'll know when you've come to it.'

His smile is as bright as his hair. He's so nonchalant about all this, and it seems so normal. Maybe to him, this is normal. And hell, I invited him over to do a reading. I have come this far. It could be utter nonsense, or maybe there's something to it. There is only one way to find out.

So I do as I'm told and wave my hand over the cards. My hand goes over all the cards three or four times before I feel a certain "pull" towards one. I stop and place my hand over it.

'Go 'head Pull it out and let's have a look at it. Oh, and remember Kim, these images aren't meant to be taken literally. There's a lot to interpreting the cards.'

A lump forms in my throat. No, a lump isn't quite what I'm going for. It's more of a tightness to it. I take a deep breath, and pull out the card, and turn it face up. My eyes skim over the image. A lightning struck tower. Flames spray outwards from the windows. And two individuals one male, and one female appear to have leaped from it. My mouth goes dry. I do not like the look of this card.

'I think I've made a mistake.' I say as I hand the card to Trevor.

'Ah, The Tower... Interesting. I don't think you've made a mistake. It's like I said, some of these cards look far worse than what they actually mean.'

He places the card down on the table, eyes skimming it over.

'Though it is curious that this is the one you chose. I must admit, I wasn't expecting that to be your card.'

'So have I made a mistake, then?'

'No.' Trevor casts me a reassuring smile and puts his hand on my shoulder. 'It's just unexpected.'

'So, what does it mean?'

'The tower, as I'm sure you can tell, looks forbidding at first glance. But with Tarot, the reader has to look beyond the depiction. In the upright position it can represent change. And you've gone through quite a bit of change, Kim.'

'It's really that simple?' It's a relief. I don't have to fear that the house will be struck by lightning and catch fire.

Trever hesitates. 'The Tower also represents the death of a loved one. But with every negative, there is a positive. A light at the end of the tunnel so to speak.'

'And that would be?'

'Change can lead to a journey of self improvement.'

That wasn't the answer I expected, but I suppose everyone could do with a fair bit of elf improvement. And I know I can't sulk forever. It's not good for anyone. Whatever path fate or whatever has in store for me, for all of us, I must learn to keep my head held high. Not everything is so terrible.

'After every storm, a rainbow appears?'

'Now you're getting it! You catch on pretty quick, yeah?'

I tuck a strand of hair behind my ear and shrug.

'I suppose I do.'

◆ ◆ ◆

Kev sits beside me on the couch. Annie is on the floor with paper and crayons.

'You're becoming quite the artist.' Laura remarks as she places her clipboard down on the desk and kneels down beside our sister. I hadn't been giving what she was doodling much thought. I'd been concentrating more on the questions the doctor asked. 'What are these though?'

Both Kevin and I lean closer to look over at the drawing. There's the house, and the three of us. Mum and Dad are among the clouds with yellow halos above their heads. But back towards the house, there are more. At first, I thought the scribbles had intended to be a representation of Toby.

'That's my friend, Emma.'

Laura smiles. 'Why is she red and Blue?'

'She cries a lot. You didn't have any red Crayons, so I used orange.'

Kevin stares at me, wide eyes that narrow to curious slits as he messes with his cricket cap. She keeps mentioning that name. We'd assumed Emma was her creation. Now, i'm not so sure. Maybe Kevin will start believing me now.

'And where did you meet Emma?' Laura's voice is calm and collected as usual. I wish I could be that calm. My heart is racing. No, no. This isn't what I wanted. I did my best to keep everything away from Annie. Then I remember that day with Lizzy. Branson called it "the spooky house." Damn that kid and his mouth. Corrupting my sisters thoughts!

'She comes into my room sometimes. Kevin lives in her sister's room. Her sister isn't very nice.'

Laura tilts her head at the two of us. As if Emma is supposed to be some representation of me. Ave I was neglecting her too much? Does she think I've been abusing her or something? What on earth could give her that idea?

I ruffle her hair. 'I'm sorry I haven't been home a lot. Do you think I'm mean to you?'

She blinks up at me and hesitates before shaking her head. 'No. But the lady that makes the rooms cold is very mean. '

This can't be happening. There's no way that this is actually my life right now. I'm not living in a haunted house. We're all just suffering from Post Traumatic Stress Disorder.

'Kim?' Laura puts a hand on my shoulder. 'You look like you're about to faint.'

'I'm alright.' A lie. I've gotten good at that as of recent, and I hate it.

KEVIN

January 2005

T he local restaurant near us has a unique theme. American Style Nineteen Fifties Diner. I'd assumed it was run by an American, but it's a Scottish bloke. Diners are uncommon, but the novelty of it draws people in, I'd wager. Trevor and I agreed to meet here. Not the first time we've met up. We were classmates in school. He'd always come to the home games. Win or lose, he always made a point to cheer on the team. On occasion I'd bring him along to the after parties. Good Lad to get pissed with. He'll show you a good time. Some were a wee bit put out by his interests. Never minded Trevor's outlandish nature, myself. He stands out, and that isn't always bad. Kim found the journal and book. She screamed like a banshee, then banned them from the house. Trevor's the type of Bloke who would fancy that type of thing.

'Nah then, Trevor!' I find him at a window booth. His hands cup a mug.

'Ey up, Kevin.' He lifts his mug towards me as I slide into a chair on the opposite end of the table and plop my messenger bag down by the floor.

'Reckon you'd fancy a look at these. Kim saw and practically brayed me.' The book is the first thing to come out. As

I'm searching for the journal, I hear him flipping through the pages.

'You ought to be mindful of this,' Trevor warns. When I look up at him, he's scanning me over, and squints as he looks over my face.

'Is it moldy?'

'No, this is a book of shadows. Not just any old spells. Blood magic. Have you been feeling okay? Blackouts, or anything like that?'

'The only thing that's a bit off is that I wake up with a few grey hairs? Not that unusual.'

Trevor looks at the journal. 'What's that?'

'A Diary it seems. Annie was insistent we didn't leave without it.'

'Your sister?'

'Aye. She kept saying she wanted to go to the old house. Hadn't the foggiest idea what she meant. Turns out that place by the church had some relics from the past, eh?' I slide it over to hm. 'Most of it is legible. From what I can tell, it belonged to a pregnant woman. Can't find a name though. Dunno what became of her. The last entry is sometime in December if I recall.'

I watch as his fingers linger in the air, before he returns them to the mug.

'Has Annie touched it? Or anyone else?'

'Annie has briefly.?'

'You might have something attached to you. She could too. Keep an eye on her. Children are prone to possession.'

I almost choke on my tea. 'Come again?'

'Children can get attached to spirits more easily. They have a way with 'em.'

'I reckon I'd know if my sister was having tea parties with ghosty goos,' I laugh and wink before taking a bite of my burger.' Oh, come off it. The house has so many stories bout it. You can't possibly believe in them all.'

'Not all,' Trevor concedes nodding his head. 'But there

must be a bit of truth to it, eh?' He holds up a finger before rummaging through his own bag. 'I've been doing some digging about the history of your house. Lots of comings and goings.'

'That place is always for sale. Kim's convinced its haunted by some sort of demonic presence or something of the sort.' It's hard not to laugh. Kim's usually the logical one.

'Do the names Sarah or Emma ever appear in this?' He nods towards the diary on the table.

I stare at him for a moment before nodding. Trevor leans forward in his chair, and slides some papers across the table for me. The one on top is a copy of a newspaper article.

Two sisters found dead on North Troy Hill. 18 December, 1832. Trevor catches my eye as I skim over the other titles. Lots of them revolve around the arrest of a local doctor. He claims he had nothing to do with it. Sounds like a fair suspect to me, but that still doesn't make me believe my house is haunted. No wonder the place is the talk of the town. Trevor turn back to the book, and flips to the front. His jaw falls open when he reads the initials scribbled I the front. The colour drains from his face as he slides an article my way.

'She was accused of witchcraft.He stares up at me again, and frowns. 'Are you positive there aren't any gaps in your memory?'

'Positive.'

He taps a new pack of cigarettes on the edge of the table. 'Alright.'

EMMA

December 1893

O ne moment I'm sitting down with tea, and the next a cloth is pressed to my mouth and nose. In my panic I inhale deeply. My head spins, but I fight. My elbow makes contact with something, but it's not enough to push my attacker away. The corset she wears absorbs most of the blow.

'I'm only trying to help you, Emma.' A voice coos. In a fog, I can't place it, but it sounds familiar. And my body goes limp. I'm tired. So very tired. How am I to defend myself as the world fogs around me? I can't hold my breath for much longer. My body screams for air, and forces an intake of breath. At first, the taste is sweet, but then as it makes its way down my throat it alters to a flavour reminiscent of candle oil. The hand only clamps tighter around my mouth and nose. I can't breathe. My vision is so foggy I can't even see the wall in front of me.

'That's it, just relax.' My body goes limp, and the last thing I remember is being lifted onto a cart before the world goes dark.

When I wake I'm on a bed. I can hear voices, but they sound muffled. A baby cries somewhere. But I don't know where. Everything feels so strange. Everything looks strange and my eyes burn. My body trembles. It's so cold. Why is it so cold? It's at that moment I realise I'm underwater?

I sit straight up, gasping for air. It's freezing. I look down to see myself surrounded In a pool of red. My stomach aches. I look down to see a hole in my stomach. Someone has cut me open, and where is my baby? With caution I step out of the tub. The hole in my stomach needs to be stitched. I reach into my pocket. I look about the room only to find rags and cloths. That'll have to do until I can get to a doctor. The baby cries louder and I can hear voices as I wrap the rags tightly around the wound. It's uncomfortable, but I don't see much of another option.

'Shh, hush now little one.'

It's the voice of my sister. What is she doing? Why does she have my baby? Why did she leave me in a tub? She should know better.

'Sarah?'

Her head jerks up. She has the baby in her arms and A bottle in his mouth.

'You're alive?'

That's the question she asks as I shiver and bleed all over the floor?

'Can I have the baby? How are they? Is it a boy? Are they healthy?' I take a step forward but something shiny catches my eye. Sarah is holding a knife.

'Don't come any closer. I don't know how you're alive but I'll let you live if you give up the baby.'

'What?'

I'm dazed and lightheaded. I need help. Can I find help? What will Sarah do to me with that knife if I try to run? Too many questions. Too many things I don't really want to know the answers to.

'But he's mine?' I lean against the wall. My head has become so heavy. And everything around me is so very light. I feel like I'm floating.

Floating.

Floating.

Floating.

And a pressure. Someone is holding something to my mouth. Sarah goes to strike me with the blade, and I raise my arms to block the blow. There's a sick ripping sound, and a burning sensation in my hand. The blade of a knife is inches from my nose. The pain hits the moment I realise what's going on, but I don't have time to stop. Despite my lightheadedness, I must go on. I pull my hand away from the blade, spraying blood everywhere. Without thinking, I run to the door clutching my bloody hand. I want to take the baby, but it would be unwise to expose him to the freezing air, and Sarah won't do any harm to him. I can go find help and get him back later.

My stomach is screaming at me to stop running. It's freezing. The exposed parts of my hair freeze to my face in an instant. I can't look back. That will only slow me down. I doubt both of them would follow Me. If I could just lead them off the trail... Because I don't dare call for help.

There's a thicket that leads to a denser part of the forest with pine trees. All I have to do is stay hidden. And find something to wrap around my hand.

I almost slip on ice, but manage to steady myself. I don't know how I manage to stay upright. Survival instincts perhaps? I duck behind a tree and let my knees give out. The bonnet on my head will have to do. To go on outside without a head cover is considered indecent, but I can't trouble myself with that at the moment. I just need to not pass out.

KIM

March 2005

Rain pounds on the roof as the thunder roars. Annie is curled up beside me. Even in the best of times, she never likes storms. And in this place, where shadows could be real or fake, it only increases her anxiety.

'It's alright, Little Dove.'

I hold her close to me, but her eyes are transfixed on the ceiling.

'Someone needs to let her out.' She murmurs into my shoulder.

'Let who out?

'Emma. She's scared of storms, too.'

Toby hasn't sat still for more than five minutes. He keeps prowling around the door. And running to the attic. Hissing at things that even Annie can't see. I'm not sure if that should be a comfort to the both of us or not.

'Toby never hisses. 'The mean lady is here.'

I shut my eyes. In my head I can hear her too. Or maybe

it's not just a voice in my head. I dunno. All I know is its loud and laughing. Toby keeps finding dead things. At least three birds flew into my window today. One was lucky and seemed only stunned. Or at least I hope that's the case. It was able to get up and fly. But did that imply it survived? There were too many questions unanswered, and all of them I don't want the answers to.

'How about we go see Kevin?'

She hesitates for a moment, but nods. I kiss the top of her head and begin humming. It will distract both of us. My pitch is less than ideal, but it's the only thing I can think to do.Thunder crashes and a bolt of lightning reflects off the window and onto my floor. Creating shadows of jagged lines. Creating an illusion of cracks in the floorboards. Annie trembles in my arms while tears stain her cheeks.

'You're with me,' I whisper. 'You're safe.'

The bedroom door seems like it's miles away. Lights begin flickering and I hear Kevin curse from the next door over. Poor bloke probably lost his work. Save as frequently as you can. That's what Dad always said.

'Kevin, we're coming by you, alright?'

A floorboard squeaks and this unholy scream shakes the house.

Annie screams, and she's full on sobbing now.

I jog over to the door, and right before my fingers can brush the knob the door slams shut.

It's actually hail that's hitting the roof. I turn to look out the window to see the snow being picked up by the gusts of wind. This place is weird.

'Kevin!' I tug on the doorknob. The stupid thing won't turn.

'Kevin we're stuck in here!'

It seems the more I tug on the door the more stuck it becomes.

'Oh bugger!' My heart thuds. 'Get us out of here!'

That chill in the air creeps up my spine.

'No, no, no, no, no.' More tugging. This door doesn't even have a lock. Why the bloody hell won't it open.?A gust of wind strong enough to open the window. Wood splinters everywhere as the shutters make contact with the wall.

'Go before she takes notice.' Someone whispers. 'You're not safe here!'

I turn to see a woman floating over by the window. Her face is shrouded in shadow. It's so cold. I snatch two sweatshirts from the drawer. Our rooms are on the second floor, but it's not that high a drop.

'Annie, hold on tight to me okay?'

She nods, and before I have the chance to lose my nerve, we jump.

EMMA

December 1893

I t's so cold, even my clothing has begun to freeze to my body. My teeth chatter. I need warmth, and a change of clothes. A doctor would also be rather lovely. Anyone at all who isn't my sister, really would be a great deal of help. To do that, I need to find my way out of these woods.

'Emma,' Sarah cackles. Her voice doesn't sound too near. I run to a bush, and crouch down, careful not to snap any twigs that may be nearby. In between the branches, a shadow emerges. She's carrying a lantern, and the smile on her face is twisted. A hand comes to my mouth as I attempt to mute my ragged breathing, and chattering teeth.

Cold. It's so cold. Almost all consuming, mind numbing even. It's taking all of my energy to not just lay down and sleep. If they weren't frozen to my face, my eyelids would be drooping. The lantern's glow comes into view. What has gotten into her? Why does she want my baby so badly when hers will be here in a short while? Slowly, I back away hoping to remain in the shadows.

'Come out, sweet thing.' There's something being illuminated by the burning candle. It's a hint of silver. The knife she plans to kill me with.

'This won't hurt. All your pain will be gone. And your boy will be in safe hands. I promise.'

Does Sarah believe me a coward or a fool? One must not give herself willingly, or they will forever be condemned to damnation. Never to be welcomed into God's domain. She reads the scriptures, she must know that. Perhaps in her madness she has forgotten.

The more I back away, the more faint her voice becomes. I look up towards the sky, even in the dark, I can make out how cloudy the sky is. The snow falls on my face, and slides down my nose and cheeks, but my body cannot feel it. Like the rest of me, it's gone numb.

I don't know how far I've walked to arrive to this place, but it's a house. There is a faint light. So it cannot be all that vacant. My boots leave tracks in the snow, and it takes all my effort to raise my hand to the door. There's a knocker, and with the last of my strength I let it fall.

A man answers. 'Who is knocking at this hour?' the breath catches in his throat as I stumble into his arms.

'My dear lady, what has happened to you?' He kneels and lifts me into his arms.

'Please,' I plead as I'm carried inside. 'I need help.'

'Stay by the fire. I'll call for a doctor.' Something is

wrapped around my shoulders. It's so heavy, I have to clutch it with both of my hands just to keep it draped around me. My body warms, but also stings. It must be safe to sleep now. My eyes shut, and even with my body stinging, sweet sleep takes me.

◆ ◆ ◆

The door squeaks open. Then there's another sharp pain in my shoulder. My eyes burst open and I see Sarah standing over me, knife in hand, fresh with blood as it drips to the floor.

'Found you,' She taunts, as she attempts to bring the blade down again. Instincts bring my foot up and kick her away. My heel makes contact with her hand and there's a loud crack. Sarah's wrist is bent at an odd angle. The knife falls to the floor, and as she screams I flee into the night once more with the knife in hand. There's a river in the back. I go to cross, but the ice cracks under my weight. Panicked, I glance over my shoulder. Sarah is running towards me. Her unbroken hand is outstretched towards me, but she slips on a bit of snow. Sarah's hand wraps around my throat, cutting off my air. I don't know what else to do, so I raise the blade, and with all my might impale her in the jaw. As it enters, it feels like cutting into raw meat. Like skinning an animal for its furs. I'm not able to look at her as she falls. In a panic, I straddle her back, and hold her head under the icy water until she stops moving.

'What have I done?' She's dead. She's dead. Oh, Jesus forgive me, for I did not mean for this to happen. I stare down at my hands. They're covered in blood. Warm blood. Sarah's blood. I have murdered my sister, Oh lord please forgive me. For I have sinned!

A hand is on my shoulder. It makes me jump.

'Easy Love.' It is the same man who carried me in. 'That was the woman who did this to you, was it not?'

Tears freeze to my face again, and another man picks me up.

'Please, someone fetch my baby.'

'Where is he?'

'A cabin in the forest.' My body is shivering again.

'We need to get her indoors.' An unfamiliar voice. My head spins. 'She'll need stitches if there is any hope for her.'

My head slumps up against the strangers chest. Out of the corner of my eye, I see Sarah's body lying in the snow. Blood pools from her cheek, staining the snow red.

'I'm sorry. I had to.' I sniff.

'You were only defending yourself, love.' The man says. It doesn't offer me any comfort. Self defence or not, Sarah was my sister. She was Ill in the head. If she had been mentally sound, I know she wouldn't have attacked me. That's just not her.

Once again the warmth of the fire wraps around me. As my eyes begin to close.

'The baby,' I whisper. 'Please bring me my baby. Cabin. Forest…. Please.'

A light begins to shine. Their voices sound so muffled. Why

do they sound so far away? The two men are so close. I can see them, even through the light. It's as though I'm in the tub again. The strength within me weakens. There's no threat anymore. It is okay. I can sleep.

Sleep.

Someone is holding my baby. I can't tell if it's the doctor, or my saviour. I reach out, but my body feels as light as air.

'May I hold him?'

The two men act as if I haven't spoken at all.

'Poor woman. She had a lot of fight in her, too.'

'Emma. My name is Emma.'

Once again, there is no response. Desperate, I reach out and go to tuck my hand under my sleeping baby boy. My hands go right through him.

'What?' This has to be a dream brought on by the cold. There's a sheet on the floor, covering something. At first, I assume it's my sister. She's calling me. But how is that possible? She's gone. I shouldn't be able to hear her voice. A set of stairs sits in the corner. Sarah's voice sounds like it's coming from a room upstairs. The man is a doctor. He probably revived her!

I hurry towards the door, and slide right through the door.

'You killed me. And now we're stuck here. The ritual failed.'

'But the doctor revived you?'

Sarah scoffs and crosses her arms.

'You always were an overly trustworthy fool. You don't realise it do you?'

No....

I'm dead, aren't I?

As I glance around, I see we're in a bedroom.

'You take the Attic. That will be your space. This one will be mine. Seeing as this whole situation is your doing, I think I should have my pick of the home And we should stay away from one another.'

KIM

After the Jump

I hold tight to Annie as we run to the car.

'Annie, get in the car. I'm going to go and get the keys, and Kevin, okay?'

She doesn't hesitate; she just sits down and pulls the sweatshirt over her head. It's much too large for her, but it's better than nothing at all.

It's not safe here lingers in my head. What did that mean? And would this only last until the storm passed? I've never seen them this active before. I kiss Annie's forehead and shut the door before I run to the front door.

'Kevin,' I call through the front door. 'We're leaving! Get down here!'

Not waiting for a reply, I jog to the kitchen and grab the keys, and make a mental note to take our jackets on the way out.

Toby skids across the floor, his whole body fluffed. He

seems frazzled as he limps over to me. He's hurt. Oh dear god, please don't let him be hurt too badly.

'C'mon Toby.' I don't remember picking him up, but he's in my arms and licking the edge of my thumb. There's a thud on the steps and he hisses loudly, but doesn't dare move.

'Kev, are you alright?'

'Just. Brilliant.'

There's something strange in the way it comes out. It's his voice, but not his accent. It's too posh to be his accent.

'Kevin?'

There's a swishing sound and I duck just in time to evade the swing of the bat. He's laughing. But it's not his laugh.

'The ones who don't believe are always the easiest to take over.' Kevin's grinning and swinging like a madman. His movements are erratic, and he lacks the proper technique of an effective swing. Toby hisses again and bats out at it with a crooked paw.

'Mangy animal!' Another swing that we manage to dodge.

'Leave them be, Sarah! Another voice shouts. There's something in front of me, blurring my vision slightly. It's the woman that opened my window. There's a slit in her stomach, and I notice a wound in her hand as she puts her arms out, as if protecting us.

'I told you to get off the property!' She snaps, it's not unkind, but more concerned.'We cannot leave this place. Go!

'What about Kevin?'

'Go!'

I obey this time, holding toby close to me, I don't stop. I

don't even think about what might happen. My main concern is Annie. Annie and Toby.Kevin is fast, but I'm faster somehow. Maybe he's fighting her. I don't know. Annie pushes open the drivers side, and I place Toby in her lap.

'What's wrong with Kevin?' Se streaks and strokes Toby. As if he's her only source of comfort. Maybe he is.

'He's possessed!' I lock the door, and buckle my seatbelt before jamming the key in the ignition, and speeding off. I don't slow down until the house is out of view. At a light, I give Lizzy a ring.

'Lizzy? Are you home right now?'

'Yeah. Are you alright? Is everything okay?'

I bite my lip. I'm not sure how to answer.

'I need you to watch Annie for a bit. And if you can, Toby needs a vet. He's hurt. I'll explain more when I get there.'

'Oh! Yeah. Uh. Sure Kim.'

'Thanks.'

'I love you.'

'I love you, too.' I hang up.

'We left Kevin.' Annie sobs in the back seat.

'I'm going back for him, don't you worry. I would never leave him behind forever. We all stick together, yeah?'

She nods and kisses Toby's head.

When we arrive, Lizzy I outside with a carrier. How she knew I'd need one I don't know? Did I tell her? I don't remember telling her. Either way, it doesn't matter. The point is the both of them will be safe.

'Be good for Lizzy, Annie.'

I kiss her on the head and give her a reassuring smile.

'Everything is going to be fine, I promise.'

I turn back to go to the car, But Lizzy stops me.

'What the hell is going on, Kim? Where's Kevin?'

'He's possessed.' I say, as if that's supposed to offer her any comfort. 'I have to go get Trevor. He'll know what to do!'

Before leaving, I turn and kiss her, smudging her red lipstick. She stares at me blankly.

'It sounds absolutely mental I know. But please. Just. Just take care of them.'

'Kim!'

I don't turn around or stop this time, I just get in the car and pray that Trevor is home.

Trevor leads me into his dining room. Scattered all across the table are papers, and various tarot cards. He must have multiple decks because each card looks drastically different from the next. There's the pleasant smell of lavender coming from a candle in the centre of the table, and it intermingles with the strong smell of the sage next to it.

'I've been looking into that house, and the rumours surrounding it.' He indicates for me to sit down, but I shake my head.

'We need to go help my brother. Trevor can you explain all of this once we know he's safe?'

He chews his lip, but nods as he grabs his keys, and a backpack.

'Let's go ghost hunting.'

There's determination in his eyes. I can't tell if he's fascinated, or terrified. For all I know, he could be both.

Back at my house, the snow falls faster. It's covered the road in patches of white. I hope there's no ice. As the wipers cast away the snowflakes, I think of Mum and Dad. How dark it was that night, as the rain poured down, how dim the streetlights must have been. The truck driver who hit their car... I hated him so much. But as I drive in this weather, I can see how the mistake was made. Maybe it's time I let go of my resentment. I can't forgive him for taking my parents, but I can at the very least admit that he never meant it.I couldn't look him in the eyes at court. I didn't care how many times he said he was sorry, or how bad the weather was. I hoped the guilt would be so bad that he killed himself. But those are the thoughts of a grieving daughter. Not what I actually wish for him. After all, the man is a father himself. I wouldn't wish this on any family.

'Kim?' Trevor drags me from my thoughts. 'Are you listening?'

'Oh.' The blood rushes to my cheeks. 'Sorry, no. Can you repeat that, please?'

'I said that I think I know why so many animals are dying on the property.'

'Yeah, it is really unsettling.'

'Their trying to escape. I don't know if it's some sort of spirit-binding, or a sacrifice, or hell. Maybe They're even trying to flee the property via the animals. I dunno. Just a theory though.'

'That's... Actually a decent thought. Did you find anything out about the history of the place?'

'No, but around this time in 1893 two women disappeared. Both were pregnant. Or so the records show.'

My mind flashes back to the woman who helped us escape. Her stomach was bleeding. Could that have symbolised the baby?

'Is that where the baby rumours come from?'

Trevor shrugs.'That would make the most sense.'

I don't dare take my eyes off the road, so I can't turn to look at him as we pull into the driveway. I take a deep breath and shut my eyes. Do this for Kevin. Now is not the time for fear. It is a time to claim my home. *Our* home.

A hand is on my shoulder, and I turn to see Trever. His face is pale, but he's still smiling.

'Whatever we must face, we will do it together.'

I don't know him well, but he is the only one that I feel confident can help me.

'You said the women went missing. Were the bodies ever found?'

He opens his mouth to reply, but instead his eye catches something and he hurries out of the car. Intrigued and anxious to find my brother, I follow suit. I'm about to run towards the door, but Trevor holds out an arm, and points to the middle of the yard.

Birds of various species, shapes, and sizes litter the ground.

'What the hell is it with this place?'

Trevor squints and tilts his head thoughtfully before spinning round and grabbing my Brother by the wrist. The bat still in his hand.

'Get out of him!' Trevor says in a tone that's commanding, but not loud enough to be considered a shout.

'Don't hurt him!' I plead as he raises a hand to the back of Kevin's head. The bat catches the edge of his cap, and Trevor grabs hold of it with his hand and begins to drag Kevin out and away from the car.

'Kim!' Comes the voice with the cadence that is to be my brothers. 'Help me!' The tone is a mockery, and beads of sweat are forming on both of the Men's foreheads. I feel helpless. Like I should be able to help somehow.

'Ignore her, Kim!' The spirit inside my brother is fighting back. Trying to regain control over the bat in his hand. However, Trevor holds tight to it.

'This is your last time to get out willingly.' Trevor locks eyes. I gotta give him credit, he's stronger than he looks.

'And how will you rid me of him?' That cackle erupts from his mouth and the pit of my stomach sinks. Trevor glances back towards the birds. Their scattered. First, they begin at the windows. But they seem to end abruptly at the edge of the property line. He smirks as if it's confirmed something for him. Trevor gives another tug at the bat, and it's yanked hard enough for the thing to lose hold of it.

'Sorry, mate.' He says before whacking my brother in the back of the head with the edge of the bat. Kevin drops like a ton of bricks.

'Trevor what the fuck?'

Trevor grabs my hand and keeps hold of Kevin.

'Form a circle! I'll explain when this is over with.' That phrase seems to get thrown around a lot, but I'm not stupid enough to not listen to instructions. Trevor obviously has a plan which is more than I can say about myself.

'Invasion this with me, Kim!' He locks his eyes on Kevin, still out cold. 'I am surrounded by a white light. Nothing I do not permit can enter. This light fulfils me. This light protects me. I am strong. I can feel its energy surrounding us. Begone, reckless spirit. You are not welcome here.'

It seems odd, but there's a warming sensation all around me. It's as if a candle has been lit within me. For the first time since we moved, I feel more in control than ever.

'Now help me get him to the end of the drive.' He whispers in my ear. When people speak about blind faith, it's usually associated with religion. Today, as the snow falls and I shiver, I am putting my blind faith in Trevor. A man I scarcely know. But he is the only hope we have. So, I do as I'm told.

'Damn, he's heavy,' I mutter as I strain to hold his dead weight. As we near the edge of the drive, his eyes flash open. The pupils are pure black. It's startling, but that only hurries me along. He begins to wiggle and fight furiously.

'No!' The thing inside him shrieks. I only hold on to him tighter. 'I will not go!'

'You will.' Trevor demands, locking eyes again as we carry him. The screaming and fighting only continues to get worse the closer we get to being off the property line. The moment his body hits the edge of the line, his jaw opens and stretches. And a white mist begins the pour from his mouth. He's gasping and coughing. He appears to turn blue and I look from Kevin to Trevor.

'He'll be okay Kim,' he assures me as a spectral form begins to take shape in the centre of the yard. And she looks even more furious than the time I first laid eyes on her.

We set Kevin down safely in the middle of my neighbours yard. I can't imagine how rude this must be. There's no car parked in the drive. Hopefully, that means nobody is home and they won't even know that there is a twenty one year old man completely oblivious to what the fuck is going on. I toss Trevor my keys, beginning to piece together what we're doing. He nods and makes a B-line to the car. He doesn't even bother to shut the door. He just speeds the hell into the road, and into my neighbours drive.

'Get him in here.' Trever orders as he takes my brother by the hands. I take him by the ankles, and we lay him in the back seat. It's so cold, I'm tempted to leave the car running just so he has some heat. If one of us is going to be sick, I'd rather it be me. There's a flick of a lighter, and the air fills with the distinct smell of winter, and sage. I shut the door and wait for Trevor's instructions. He passes me the Sage and he begins to walk back towards the house.

'You think that little stick can stop me, boy?'

She grins at him and spins upwards towards the roof. 'C'mon,' Trevor motions towards the house before sprinting off. I follow, not really knowing what else to do. For a moment, I glance back at the car.

'Should we really just leave my brother there?'

'I don't like it either, Kim but it's the safest place for him right now. You just have to trust me!'

The storm outside only continues to rage harder. Hail thuds against the roof, and in the silence of the house it seems so much louder than it should be. Upstairs, the doors slam repeatedly and squeak open. There seems to be a scuffle of some sort going on. Somehow Trever ignores it and begins crumpling newspapers and tossing logs into the fireplace, and mutters under his breath.

'What can I do?'

'Walk around the entryway of the room with the sage. Make sure the smoke touches everything.' Even though he's a fast talker, he sounds so calm. I'm envious, but something tells me he's done stuff like this before. I walk over to the door and begin twirling the smoke in all directions. There's a flick of a match behind me, and I glance back to see him toss a match into the fireplace. He grabs his backpack, and begins to ruffle through it, muttering something I can't make out from this distance. He then tosses some sage onto the fire.

'Should cut her off from the roof at least.' He stands and dusts off his hands. There's another crashing sound coming from upstairs as Trevor flicks his backpack up and over his shoulder before he joins me again.

'Emma's defending this place, and you.'

'Trevor, the animals! The woman is trying to escape with them, right?' Does that mean a price must be paid to free them?

'That seems to be her theory at the very least. I know She practced blood magc."

'Is blood the answer' I slide a knife into my pocket when he isn't looking. If blood is the price then I will pay it.

'Sarah! I call you by your name!'

Trevor stares at me, wide eyed.

'Kim! What are you doing? Using her name gives her more power!'

A window shatters, and in a moment, Sarah is standing in front of me.

'Kimberly!' She grins, wild and wide eyes. Her eyes are pure black. I look her in the eye and pull the knife from my pocket.

'Is freedom from this home what you want?' I stare right into her eyes. I'm done running away. I'm done feeling not in control. 'This is my home, and you are not welcome here.'

Kevin's words ring out in my head again. *Blood is the answer.*

He goes to grab the knife, but he misunderstands what I intend to do. Without breaking eye contact with the now manic ghost floating in front of me, I slide the blade across my palm.

'I am a willing participant. I demand that you leave this home and my family. Begone and let your soul finally rest.'

Drops of blood fall to the floor.

'You were trapped here because of blood. Let this set you free.'

Sarah stares at my dripping hand and watches as the blood begins to pool at my feet. There is a faint glow as a light begins to shine into the floor. There is a heat. Something opens up. A black creature rises from where my blood still pools. I jump out of its way. It is huge and hooded. A bony hand reaches out towards the spectral figure and beckons to her.

'It's time.' The voice is husky. Like it spends all day inhaling smoke from a campfire.

'Where will I go?' Sarah demands, holding her hand.

'The girl has paid the toll for your selfishness.' She tries to run, but the reaper snaps his fingers and she is frozen in place.

'How!' Sarah's eyes fix on the cloak as it flaps around the floor. 'Why did it work for her and not me?'

'The sacrifice must be willing.' He snaps again, and flames rise higher. Trevor and I watch, stunned by what we're witnessing. There was all just a lucky guess. I did this thinking that maybe she only felt like she was trapped here, though that is probably foolish considering she couldn't pass the property line.

'Enough.' He demands, as Sarah slowly begins to float towards the portal in the floor.

'Emma!' Her fingers claw at the floor, but they only slide through the wood. Just like that, the both of them are gone. And what once was a gaping hole in the floor is now wood. No more heat, or unholy screams. Just me and Trevor, staring with our mouths agape trying to process what the fuck just happened.

'How did you know to do that?'

'I...Didn't.'

The door to the attic opens up a crack. I blow out the sage and walk into the room. Sure enough, Emma sits there.

And the skirts of her dress just barely brush the floor.

'That was quick thinking, Kim.'

Something is being pressed into the wound of my hand. Trevor has pulled a wrap from his backpack and is staring at me in a stunned silence as he wraps it up.

'I just wanted my house back.' I don't know what else to say. Ema smiles, and places a hand to my cheek. 'Does this mean you wish for me to go as well?'

Her face is so soft, but I can see the resemblance now that I'm able to see her cup close.

'Only if you want to.'

She courtesies to me. 'If you do not mind, I would like to remain here for a time. If only for a little longer. I do rather enjoy playing with your sister.'

'And from my understanding, she enjoys playing with you as well.-- Thank you for protecting us.'

She bows her head. 'Then I will remain.'

KEVIN

An hour later

'Take it easy,' Trevor says, sliding an arm under me. 'That's it. Nice and slow.'

'I should have listened.' I rub my head where he struck me. The Doctors cleared me. No concussion. Just a broken ankle and some bruising. A nurse walks over with a pair of crutches. My arms are sore just thinking about how exhausting these next two weeks will be having to climb the staircase.

'We live and we learn.' He makes sure I'm steady before letting me go.

'It was good of you to say with me while Kim went to get Annie and Toby.'

'I don't mind. Wanted to make sure you were alright anyway.' We can start a club, Toby and I. The Busted leg club. From the sounds of it, he'll make a full recovery. Thank God, I'd never forgive myself if something worse happened. Toby's getting on in years but he still has lots of life in him. Trevor walks over to a bench and pats the spot next to him. We'll be able to see Km's car when she pulls in. Trevor passes me my cap.

'The Gray doesn't look bad on you at least. It adds a wee bit of character if you ask me.'

'It'll be a good story to tell at parties.' We both chuckle. Trevor leans forward and looks at me.

'You're alright though, eh Kevin?'

'I haven't really thought 'bout it. A lot to take in, yeah?' He nods and squeezes my shoulder before he lets his hand drop. I smile to reassure Trevor that the gesture wasn't un-welcome.

'Gives me an idea though. Kim won't fancy it, but you might, eh? You still have those cards?"

'Always!'

'Fancy a business partner?'

'Depends,' Trevor hums but the concern is replaced with a familiar glint of curiosity. 'What do you have in mind?'

EMMA

January 2007

I n the two hundred years since the house was built, families come and go, but one thing always remains the same. They never stay. Old Victorian homes often hold rumours and legends make the rounds about town. On stormy nights, it's said the cry of a baby, and a woman's screams can be heard. It's really quite good for business.

A cordless object makes a terrible Racket made up of loud, high pitched, ringing noises. Trevor insists it's called a "phone" and the noise it omits is Für Elise. The piece is almost unrecognizable to my ears.

'The Attic Explorations,' Kevin says from a desk in the corner. 'We're the attic crew, paranormal investigators with tarot too!' The slogan is a bit much, but it does seem to be effective. This is the longest anyone has ever stayed here, and I rather enjoy the company. The people who pass through and ask invasive questions, I could do without. However, I understand that Kevin and Trevor have a business to run. At least they were polite enough to ask.

'I'll have to check our availability, but yes I believe my

partner and I could make the trip.' He pulls open a drawer, and begins scribbling on some paper.

I smile. They've come far in a short amount of time. Kim wants no part in this business, but when Trevor and Kevin came to them with the idea she told them, 'I'm not keen on being involved. Give it a go if you think you'll be happier with this, rather than the Cinema.' His hair has gone a bit grey. Most of it s my sisters doing.

When patrons come for a visit, they are always sure to give me my space, which am entirely grateful for. The agreement we had was people were allowed to ask questions, but the Attic would be what they call an office space, and off limits to any visitors they might receive for a Tarot reading.

'Oi, Trevor!' Kevin stands, taking the paper with him. 'We've got rumours of a ghostly choir in Fountains Abbey.' He pauses at the door to offer a smile before removing his cap, and nodding towards me.

'Apologies for the disturbance, Miss Emma.'

'I understand. Off you go.' I wave a hand at him, and return to the window. The weather is gloomy. Rain rolls down the windows. Weather such as this used to frighten me. I don't allow it to trouble me anymore. On occasion, I consider moving on from this place. Since I am no longer bound to the house, sometimes I take the air at night. Beckton has changed so much since I've walked the streets. Really, it's rather fascinating to see it all now that I have the freedom to do so.

Without Sarah here to torment, everyone is much more relaxed. Turning round I look towards the walls. The wallpaper is still the same as it were when I Arrived. An echo of

B.L. Koller

what still remains of the Victorians that came before. My time will come as well.

'Soon' I whisper to the damaged wallpaper. 'Now is not yet the time.'

A WORD OF THANKS

Hello dear reader. I hope you enjoyed reading Rumours as much as I loved writing it! What started off as an experiment, turned into what you just read. Kim was one of the most difficult characters to write, but she soon became one of my favourites! It's hard for me to believe that at one point, we saw this story only through her eyes, and it was just about a girl who was apprehensive to move out of her parents' home, and go to University. She had other ideas when I sat down to write.
I also want to thank the incredible support system I have. Matt, without you I wouldn't have the confidence to put this out. Devin, without you getting me into horror RFTA would have been something very different. To think that this whole project was just going to be 3000 words total. How it became a Haunted house story, written in first person present tense, and over 16k I'm not sure. I'm happy it did! I hope you are too. Peter, you've always been a huge support system, no matter how out there my ideas are. The support of those around you can be an amazing motivation on the bad days, and give you the extra drive on your good.

If you could please take the time to leave a review, that would be so very helpful.
Thank you,

A FIRST LOOK
AT SPIRITS OF
BECKTON BOOK II:

Whispers From The Clock Tower

Coming this Autumn to Amazon Kindle and Paperback.
This is just a preview chapter and is subject to change. Enjoy this first hand look at how Beckton has changed ten years later.

KEVIN

The Diner

Our town, Beckton has an unusual reputation. It was founded in the late seventeen hundreds as a small farming town in Yorkshire England. Or so that's what they say. Those who know better, understand why the locals affectionately refer to the town as "Bloody Beckton." Once upon a time, there were Covens all throughout this town. What remains of the original Coven is said to be unknown. My family knows better. We know how powerful these witches once were, and the danger they can still impose. I'm reminded of this every time I look at myself in the mirror. A permanent mark that Beckton has left on me. When people ask how I've greyed so early, I give them the simple answer.

'Oh, it's just genetics.' Which in part, may be a half truth. Dad started to go grey in his early twenties, but my circumstances for salt and pepper hair are far more sinister. A permanent reminder o my failure listen. To sum it up in one sentence, I was possessed by a ghost that had been trapped in my house for two hundred years. Sarah was a wee bit stir crazy. Or mad. Bit of both. Her sister Emma assures me she wasn't all that mentally sound in life. Reckon that's why she fancied the idea of joining one of these covens, and practiced blood magic. The most dangerous kind, according to my partner, Trevor. Back then, I didn't believe him. I didn't believe in any of it. I thought they were just rumors. I was wrong.

'Still with us, Kev?' Trevor asks when he stops the car at the light.

'Aye, just thinking.'

'About our new assignment?'

'Nah. The house. How stupid I was.'

When we first moved to Beckton ten years ago, I never would've seen myself in the Ghost hunting business, now I can't picture life witthout it.

I glance back out the car window. We pass the remnants of what once was a house. Still standing, despite the fire.

'I've been thinking about having another look around in that wall.' Trevor says. 'Those missing pages must be somewhere.'

'Have fun. I ain't going near that place. I have enough grey hairs for this life time.'

'I think your hair adds character.' He smiles.

'Says the one who puts neon green dye in his conditioner.' That's one of the many things I love about Trevor. Whatever adventure he partakes in, he dedicates himself to.

I glance at the clock on the dashboard.

'Fancy paying Kim a visit? School should be out soon, and that means the rush will have her tearing her hair out in the walk in. Seeing our bright smiling faces might lift her spirits.'

'Sure! I'm starving.'

Nineteen fifties music pours out from the speakers. The whole aestetic of this place is like walking back in time. Even the waiter and waitress uniforms make one feel like they've just returned from a sock hop.

'Hello!' My twin sister says as the little bell on the door jingles. 'Oh it's you lot.'

'Ey up, sis.' I lean over and kiss her cheek. 'How you holding up?'

'It hasn't been too bad today.' She takes two menus out and leads us towards a booth. 'How was St. George's Asylum tour?'

'We still have to review the audio,, but my hopes are not high.' Trevor takes a seat opposite me. 'Wild goose chase?'

'Seems like it.' He mutters as Kim leaves to get two coffee mugs. Really, we don't even need the menus. Kim knows our orders by heart by now.

'They want us to do a sweep of the place at night. Supposedly, thats when everyone is most active.' I say as she returns with the fresh cups of coffee.

'Trev, all that sugar is going to rot your teeth you know.' This is already his third cup of coffee today.

'I have excellent dental hygiene,' He quips as he dumps three sugar packets into the piping hot mug. 'But thank you for the concern.'

Kim shakes her head and sighs. 'The usual, then?'

We both nod as Trevor stirs his coffee. By the time Kim returns with our soup orders, Trevor has already finished more than half. His caffeine addiction is something I borderline envy.

Kim balances the round tray on the palm of her hand. 'The French onion for Kev.' She places it down. 'Careful it's hot. And the Chicken noodle for Trevor. With a vanilla shake topped with strawberry sauce.'

I can't help but smile when he lights up. I've seen this expression a hundred times over and yet it never gets old.

'Thank you, Kim.— oh look.' He nods towards the front door. 'Annie is here. Perfect! I wanted to tell her the good news.'

'Good news?' Kim pauses and hands trevor a red and white striped straw.

'St. George would be an excellent first hunt for her.'

Kim and I exchange a look. I shrug. She's been asking for years. St. Georges Asylum can't be any worse than our own house.

The order bell rings from the kitchen. Kim turns away. 'We'll be discussing this later.- Annie you can sit with Kevin and Trevor. I'll be right over.'

'Nah then Little Dove.' I wave to my little sister. She adjusts the bag over her shoulder. 'I'm gonna change.' She's never been one for school uniforms. And who can blame her? The school colors are navy blue and gold. A terrible combination really. Only rivaled by the hideous mascot. A blue and gold, cheap looking Raven. A nod to the towns history.

Her friend Branson follows behind her. His classic crooked smirk etched on his face. If you didn't know him well, this could be mistaken for cockiness or arrogance. While at times, he can be both, it's simply his goofy default expression. He gave a quick smile, and a wee before heading over to the kitchen.

'Don't be a stranger, lad!' Trevor calls 'join us.' Trevor calls, making him pause at the door.. He pokes his head in, exchanges some words with someone.inside, and jogs over to our table.

'I wouldn't wanna impose..'

'It's not imposing if you're invited.' I chuckle as Trevor moves over to make room at the booth. And pats the seat next to him.

'I gotta go and have a chat with Dahv, but I'll join you after? Delivery shipment related.'

'Aye, but come back when you're finished. Don't let Kim scare you away.'

He laughs. 'If it was that easy, Annie would be at my house more often.' He winks and gives us a wave. 'I'll see you in a bit, thank you.'

I've always liked Branson. He's a good kid. At times, can be a little rebellious, but what eighteen year old doesn't show tiny hints of rebellion?

Annie remerges from the bog, now in her casual clothes and sits down. 'How was the tour of St. George?'

'Seemingly a gimmick.' Trevor sighs. 'But we've been assigned to check the place out at night. Want to come?'.

Theres a glimmer in her eye. We've always let her help with business. The simple stuff like reviewing audio and video. She's never been on a hunt though. Kim never fails to come up with some excuse. 'Are yo serious?'

'Serious as we can be.' I grin.

'Aye! Course I wanna go!'

' It's next Saturday.' I fix her with a knowing look and raise a brow. 'Are you willing to give up a night of partying?'

'For a hunt,' Annie beams. 'I'd give up just about anything.'

'Careful,' Trevor warns. 'Don't say that too loud. Spirits are always listening.'

I know he means this mostly in jest, but their is truth to his words. Beckton is not a town where one should be willing to sacrifice something valuable for. Theres a thinking noise, its light at first. It makes us all turn to gaze out the window. The wind has picked up, and raindrops start rolling down the diner windows.

'Ey by gum!' We hear from the kitchen. Better go shut me windows!' Branson bursts from the kitchen, and dashes out the door. Shame he shows no interest in sports. He'd be good at cricket. I turn and glance at Annie. She's watching with a small smile out the window. I can feel Trevors gaze on me. He's got his head cradled in his palm, and glances from me to Annie. I shake my head and laugh quietly into the mug. Ah to be young and fancy someone from afar again. Then there's a loud clap of thunder, and the lights begin to flicker. Trevor sits up a little straighter. A bit more alert. His fingers clamp the edge of the table. He senses something.

'Trevor?' He gets like this sometimes. I wouldn't call it a state. Definatly no where near a possession. But he sees things that we do not. "Beyond our time" he told me once. His breathing becomes slower, and deeper as he grounds himself. I know better than to interfere. Annie goes to touch him, but I stop her.

'Let it play out.' I smile at her, hoping to offer her some comfort. 'He's okay.'

This is the price of an old soul. Two lives at once. I do not have such a gift, and I'm glad for it. I doubt I'd be able to handle it.

Trevors grip loosens on the table and his eyes come back into focus.

'I need to speak with Emma.' He says. I don't press him on why. He'll tell me when the time is right.

'Is that possible?' Annie's eyes go wide. 'I thought it was impossible to talk to a ghost once they moved on'

He bites his lip. 'It's possible, but risky as all hell. Much easier for a dreamer. But I'll need someone to make sure if things go south...' He looks at me apologetically.

'Aye,' I mutter, reluctantly. 'Aye. I'll do it.'

'I want to help.' Annie quips up. Trevor and I exchanges glances, and after a moment of thinking it over, he nods. 'If she's going to join the Attic crew,' He begins. 'She must understand what she's getting into. All aspects of the paranormal. And the dangers that come with it.'

Branson's return is signaled by the bell on the door once again. Drenched from head to toe despite only being outside for at maximum a minute.

'Isn't English weather lovely?' Kim remarks in passing as Branson scoots in next to Annie. Who waves Kim over so the two of them can order.

'I'll take a cocoa, and an order of the waffles, please Kim.'

'Same. But make mine a double on the waffles.'

'Kim scribbles down the order on her note pad. dunno where you put it all, Branson.'

'Down the Bog like everyone else.'

Kim scrunches up her face and gives him the side eye. He merely beams at her, bright as he can. She rolls her eyes, and turns away. 'You're lucky you're so skinny, the way you eat.' She remarks before turning away. Something flashes in his eyes at the remark. A wince? Doubt? Something I've seen glimpses in before. He mutters something in French that I don't understand.

'Branson, you good, Mate?'

'Aye!' He's back to beaming, and wipes the wet fringe out of his eyes. 'I don't like being wet is all.'

I've known him a long time. I know he has a deep seeded fear of drowning, but a little rain never hurt anyone, yeah? He's a terrible liar, but I won't press him for the truth. He'll talk about it when the time is right.

When we arrive home, the cat is climbing up the curtains. 'Wicca!' I scold as I unhook her claws from the fabric. Her black tail is fluffed. Toby must have spooked her again. I look in the corner to see Tobys transparent form curled in his old bed. He fails to grasp the concept of "the dead don't sleep.."' But he likes to pretend. I kiss Wicca's fluffy black head and put her down. Even though Toby remains here, Kim needed a living, breathing companion to comfort her. 'Little menace you are.' I say to Toby before walking up the stairs. Even after all these years, the top step still creaks. Trevor and I walk past the bedrooms, and go right for the attic.

Walking into the attic and not feeling the chill still takes me by surprise. After Emma made the choice to pass on to the other side, the temperature of the house rose considerably. It still gets a chilly from time to time if Toby decides to make an appearance, but he takes up considerably less space than a human ghost. He lived a good life; sixteen years. And he went peacefully in his sleep. No pain, no illness—that we knew of. But he still lingers.

Theres a high pitched mew at the door.

'Aye, you can come and listen too.' I sit down at the desk chair and wait for the black cat to hop onto my lap. She's a lot smaller than Toby, even with all the extra fluff. It was Kim's idea to name her Wicca. Honestly, I'm just happy her sense of humor pops in and out every now and again. Trevor settles in at the desk next to me and begins to upload the audio to the computers via USB.

We put on out headsets and begin to listen. About an hour or so goes by with little results. Then Trevor nudges my shoulder.

'Oi Kevin.' He hi lights a bit of the audio track and increases the volume. 'What do you make of this?'

My brow furrows and I plug in my headset. It plays over again on a loop. A voice that's vaunt. Desperate to be heard from the sounds of it. Trevor and I look at each other.
'Does that sound like English to you?'
I shake my head. I'm no linguist, but it sounds like French to me.'
Trevors mouth quirks upwards. 'Looks like a job for Annie's not boyfriend. Doesn't he tutor her in French?'
'Something like that.' I mutter. 'She's growing up.' Too fast for my liking.

WHERE TO FIND
B.L. KOLLER

Newsletter:
http://eepurl.com/gxQgdr

Twitter:
https://twitter.com/BLKoller

Instagram:
https://www.instagram.com/b.l.kollerwrites/

Good Reads:
https://www.goodreads.com/author/
show/18546140.B_L_Koller

Amazon Author Page:
https://www.amazon.com/B-L-Koller/e/B07WJ6WBSL?
ref=sr_ntt_srch_lnk_1&qid=1583846742&sr=8-1

Made in the USA
Columbia, SC
23 October 2021